TO THE BIGGEST INSPIRATION IN OUR LIVES, OUR DAD.

Thanks for putting the ball in J.R.'s crib when he was a baby and always supporting us over the years.

We wouldn't be here without you, Dad.

www.mascotbooks.com

HoopSmiths: J.R. and Chris Learn Teamwork

©2018 J.R. Smith & Chris Smith. All Rights Reserved. No part of this publication may be reproduced, stored in a retrieval system or transmitted in any form by any means electronic, mechanical, or photocopying, recording or otherwise without the permission of the author.

For more information, please contact:
Mascot Books
620 Herndon Parkway #320
Herndon, VA 20170
info@mascotbooks.com

Library of Congress Control Number: 2018907587

CPSIA Code: PRT0818A
ISBN-13: 978-1-68401-997-7

Printed in the United States

HoopSmiths

J.R. AND CHRIS LEARN TEAMWORK

J.R. SMITH & CHRIS SMITH
illustrated by Kris Carter

J.R. was dribbling down the court as fast as he could. Time ticked down with every step he took. Just one more basket and his team would win the game.

"Pass it to me! Pass it to me!" Chris yelled as he ran down the court. "I'm open!"

J.R. looked over at Chris, then to the basket. *I can make it,* he thought. *I'm not passing it to my little brother!*

"PASS IT, J.R.! Pass it to Chris!" their dad yelled.

J.R. took a shot as the buzzer sounded. It was an airball. J.R. couldn't believe it. He had made that shot so many times before.

The car ride home was silent.
The boys hung their heads low.

"If you would've passed it to me, I could've made it,"
said Chris. "Way to go, *Swish.*"

"Whatever," said J.R. "You could've missed too."

"Enough," said their dad. "You boys will never make it out of the Bitty League if you don't learn how to work together as a team on the court. Even Michael Jordan is nothing without his teammates."

"AND OFF THE COURT," their dad continued. "You have to learn to work together there too. You boys are young with your futures ahead of you. I work hard as a mason every day, but you both could do so much more. Don't you boys want to play in the NBA one day?"

"Yes," they said together.

"Then you have to work together on and off the court to accomplish your goals," their dad finished.

That night after dinner, the family sat down
to watch an NBA game. It was their favorite
after-dinner activity, and J.R. and Chris always
wore their favorite jerseys. With five minutes left
on the clock, their mom turned off the TV.

"Hey!" cried J.R.

"It was tied!" cried Chris.

"It's time to do your homework, boys," she
said. "There will be other games to watch."

J.R. trudged to his room and opened his backpack. *Math.* His least favorite subject. He was working on a problem when there was a soft knock at his door.

"Come in," he said.

"Can you help me with my homework?" Chris asked.

J.R. wanted to say he was busy, but then he thought about what their dad had said earlier—
YOU HAVE TO WORK TOGETHER.

"Sure, Chris," he said. "Come on in. What do you need help with?"

Together, they worked through Chris's homework. J.R. was surprised to find he actually enjoyed it!

The next day after school, J.R. asked his dad if he could go to practice early.

"I want to practice for our championship game that's coming up," J.R. said.

"Don't you think there's someone you should include?" his dad asked.

"You're right," said J.R. "Can Chris come too?"

On the way to practice, their dad quizzed them on all the basketball trivia he could think of.

At the court, J.R. and Chris went through their drills. J.R. made sure to pass the ball to Chris, and he cheered for him after every shot he took. Then, Chris went to the three-point line and bounce passed the ball to J.R. so he could practice layups.

"GOOD WORK, BOYS!" their dad cheered. "We'll be in good shape for the championship this weekend!"

Before they knew it, it was time for the championship game. The team huddled together for the pre-game talk.

"Let's get out there and do what we do best. We practice hard every day, and now it's time to show it! J.R., Chris, you two are our starting guards today. I expect to see a lot of great teamwork! Teamwork on three!"

The team played hard in the first half. Chris passed the ball to J.R. from the three-point line like they practiced, and J.R. scored layup after layup.

"WAY TO GO, SWISH!" Chris cheered.

But the other team was just as good. For every basket the Big Earls scored, the other team answered back. When the first half ended, they were still down by eight points.

"Don't worry," said their dad. "We still have plenty of time left for a comeback. Just keep working hard and taking those shots. They're bound to go in! Let's go, Big Earls!"

"LET'S DO WHAT WE PRACTICED," J.R. told Chris as they ran back on the court.

The team gave it their all in the second half and came back to tie up the score.

In the final minutes of the game, J.R. found himself dribbling down the court.

"Pass it to me! Pass it to me!" Chris cried.

J.R. looked over at Chris, then to the basket. Then he passed the ball.

Chris shot and scored! The buzzer sounded and everyone went wild!

"WAY TO GO, CHRIS!" J.R. cheered.

"GOOD WORK, GUYS!" their dad cheered.
"I'm so proud of your hard work and determination. You guys showed a lot of heart out there, and we played together as a team. The championship is ours!"

J.R. and Chris high fived. "Our next big goal is the NBA!"

BIG EARL SAYS...

"Let's get out there and do what we do best. We practice hard every day, and now it's time to show it!"

J.R. SMITH YOUTH FOUNDATION

The J.R. Smith Youth Foundation is a New Jersey non-profit corporation. The Foundation was organized in 2006 to provide opportunities and support for young people through arts, education, sports, and other beneficial activities through scholarships, grants, and programs designed to further those goals.

A portion of the proceeds from this book will be donated to the J.R. Smith Youth Foundation.

ABOUT THE AUTHORS

Earl Joseph Smith Jr., better known as J.R. Smith, was born in New Jersey in 1985. J.R. was a star member of the St. Benedict's High School basketball team before entering the NBA Draft in 2004. He spent his first two seasons in the NBA with the then New Orleans Hornets before being traded to the Denver Nuggets in 2006. During the 2011 lockout, J.R. played in China, leading the league in scoring and making the All Star Game. He then returned to the NBA with the New York Knicks, playing alongside his brother, Chris. J.R. now plays for the Cleveland Cavaliers, with whom he won a championship with in 2016.

During the offseason, J.R. returns to his hometown of Millstone, New Jersey, with his wife and kids to be near the rest of his family and the place he calls home.

Chris Smith was born in New Jersey in 1987. Growing up, Chris was a three-sport athlete—playing basketball, football, and baseball. In high school, Chris scored over 1,300 points as a member of the Lakewood High School basketball team before finishing his career at St. Benedict's High School. Chris played college basketball for two years at Manhattan College before transferring to the University of Louisville, where he was a member of their 2012 Final Four team. Chris went on to play in the NBA for the New York Knicks with his older brother, J.R. Chris has also played professionally in Canada and Israel.

ABOUT THE ILLUSTRATOR

Kris's magical illustrations have brought many smiles to kids around the country. His work includes *F is for Finally: The Story of the 2016 Chicago Cubs*, *2 Kurious Kids*, *The Pink Panther #1 Comic Book*, and concept designs for Barehand's video game *Cede*. Kris currently lives in Massachusetts and enjoys playing sports, reading a good sci-fi book, and eating plenty of crispy, delicious shrimp. You can check out his website at kriscarterdesigns.weebly.com.